Fearsome Creatures of the Lumberwoods

With a Few Desert and Mountain Beasts

By William T. Cox

Illustrated by Coert DuBois

Washington, D. C.
Press of Judd & Detweiler, Inc.
1910

Affectionately dedicated to the Concatenated Order of Hoo-Hoo and all who know the fellowship of the woods

NO. 19949

ISBN: 978-1-6673-0441-0 paperback
ISBN: 978-1-6673-0442-7 hardcover

INTRODUCTION

Every lumber region has its lore. Thrilling tales of adventure are told in camp wherever the logger has entered the wilderness. The lumber jack is an imaginative being, and a story loses none of its interest as it is carried and repeated from one camp to another. Stories which I know to have originated on the Penobscot and the Kennebec are told, somewhat strengthened and improved, in the redwood camps of Humboldt Bay. Yarns originating among the river drivers of the Ottawa, the St. Croix, and the upper Mississippi are respun to groups of listening loggers on Vancouver Island. But every lumber district has its own peculiar tales. Some have their songs also, and nearly all have mysterious stories or vague rumors of dreadful beasts with which to regale newcomers and frighten people unfamiliar with the woods.

Much has been written concerning the lumber jack and his life; some of his songs, rough but full of the sentiment of his exciting vocation, have been commemorated, but, so far as I know, very few of the strange creatures of his imagination have ever been described by the naturalist or sketched by the artist.

The lumber regions are contracting. Stretches of forest that once seemed boundless are all but gone, and many a stream is quiet that once ran full of logs and echoed to the song of the river driver. Some say that the old type of logger himself is becoming extinct. It is my purpose in this little book to preserve at least a description and sketch of some of the interesting animals which he has originated.

WM. T. COX.

ACKNOWLEDGMENT

Grateful acknowledgment is made to the artist, Mr. Coert Du Bois, who has so faithfully represented these animals. He never could have drawn them so true to life had he not met them on tote road and trail. To Mr. George B. Sudworth, dendrologist of the Forest Service, also I am indebted for his kind assistance in classifying the animals. My thanks are due in no small measure to numerous friends among lumbermen and foresters throughout the country and in Canada for furnishing important scientific "facts" concerning these creatures their ranges and habits.

INDEX

THE HUGAG

THE HUGAG.
(Rythmopes inarticulatus.)

The hugag is a huge animal of the Lake States. Its range includes western Wisconsin, northern Minnesota, and a territory extending indefinitely northward in the Canadian wilds toward Hudson Bay. In size the hugag may be compared to the moose, and in form it somewhat resembles that animal. Very noticeable, however, are its jointless legs, which compel the animal to remain on its feet, and its long upper lip, which prevents it from grazing. If it tried that method of feeding it would simply tramp its upper lip into the dirt. Its head and neck are leathery and hairless; its strangely corrugated ears flop downward; its four-toed feet, long bushy tail, shaggy coat and general make-up give the beast an unmistakably prehistoric appearance. The hugag has a perfect mania for traveling, and few hunters who have taken up its trail ever came up with the "beast or back to camp. It is reported to keep going all day long, browsing on twigs, flopping its lip around trees, and stripping bark as occasion offers, and at night, since it cannot lie down, it leans against a tree, bracing its hind legs and marking time with its front ones. The most successful hugag hunters have adopted the practice of notching trees so that they are almost ready to fall, and when the hugag leans up against one both the tree and the animal come down. In its helpless condition it is then easily dispatched. The last one killed, so far as known, was on Turtle River, in northern Minnesota, where a young one, weighing 1,800 pounds, was found stuck in the mud. It was knocked in the head by Mike Flynn, of Cass Lake.

Page Nine

THE GUMBEROO

THE GUMBEROO.

(Megalogaster repercussus.)

In the foggy region along the Pacific Coast from Grays Harbor to Humboldt Bay there ranges a kind of creature that has caused much annoyance in the lumber woods. This is the gumberoo, which, luckily, is so rare that only once in a great while is one seen. It is believed to remain in hiding most of the time in the base of enormous, burned-out cedar trees, from where it sallies forth occasionally on frightful marauding expeditions. During these periods of activity the beast is always hungry and devours anything it can find that looks like food. A whole horse may be eaten at one sitting, distending the gumberoo out of all proportions, but failing to appease its hunger or cause it the slightest discomfort.

The specimens seen are reported to have been coal black, but that may have been due to their being smirched with the charred wood. In size the beast corresponds closely to a black bear, for which it might be mistaken only for the fact that the gumberoo is almost hairless. To be sure, it has prominent eyebrows and some long, bristly hairs on its chin, but the body is smooth, tough, and shiny and bears not even a wrinkle. The animal is a tireless traveler when looking for food, but is not swift in its movements or annoyed in the slightest degree by the presence of enemies. The latter characteristic is easily accounted for by the fact that no other animal within its range has ever found a successful method of attacking a gumberoo or a vulnerable spot in one's anatomy. Whatever strikes the beast bounds off with the same force. Its elastic hide hurls back with equal ease the charging elk and the wrathy hornet. A rock or peavey thrown at the creature bounds back at whoever threw it, and a bullet shot against its hide is sure to strike the hunter between the eyes.

It is believed that the scarcity of gumberoos is due to their combustible character and the prevalence of forest fires. The animal burns, like celluloid, with explosive force. Frequently during and after a forest fire in the heavy cedar near Coos Bay woodmen have insisted that they heard loud reports quite unlike the sound of falling trees, and detected the smell of burning rubber in the air.

Page Eleven

THE ROPERITE

THE ROPERITE.
(Rhynchoropus Aagellifonnis.)

In the foothills of the Sierras, where the Digger pine grows, dwells one of the most peculiarly specialized animals to be found anywhere on the American continent. No one knows its life-history, even approximately, and many a discussion has been based upon the question as to whether the beast is born, hatched from eggs, or comes into existence spontaneously from some mountain cavern. The Digger Indians say that roperites are the spirits of early Spanish ranchers, and blood-curdling are the tales they tell of hapless creatures pursued by the beast, snared with its marvelous rope-like beak, and dragged to death through thorny chaparral. No man or animal can hope to outrun it. It steps upon road-runners or kicks them out of the way, and no obstacle appears sufficient to stop its progress or even slacken its speed, as it seemingly half flies, half bounds across the rugged country which it inhabits. Its leathery skin is impervious to thorn and its flipper-legs uninjured by the sharpest rocks. According to A. B. Patterson, of Hot Springs, California, who saw the last roperite authentically reported, the animal has a large set of rattles on its tail, which it vibrates when in pursuit of game, thus producing a whirring sound like that of a giant rattler. The effect of this upon an animal closely pursued may be imagined. Lumbermen operating in the region between Pitt River and the southern end of the Sierras are urgently requested to make every effort to secure a living specimen of the roperite.

Page Thirteen

THE SNOLIGOSTER

THE SNOLIGOSTER.
(Dorsohastatus caudirotula.)

In the cypress swamps of the South, and particularly in the region about Lake Okechobee, Florida, woodmen tell of a strange and dangerous animal known as the snoligoster. This creature is of enormous proportions and is credited with a voracious appetite. Worst of all, its appetite is only appeased by the eating of human beings. In form the snoligoster resembles a huge crocodile, but it is covered with long, glossy fur and has no legs or fins, except one long spike on its back. A person naturally wonders how such an animal can manage to travel through the water and mud of the swamp region where it lives, but nature has provided it with a means for driving itself along. On the end of its tail are three bony plates much resembling the propeller on a steamboat. These revolve at a terrific rate, driving the animal like a torpedo boat through the mud. They servjC other purposes as well, for when a snoligoster catches an unfortunate pickaninny, or even a full-grown negro, upon which it delights to feed, it tosses the victim up and backward so as to impale him upon the spike fin, where several may be carried until sufficient for a meal have been collected. The snoligoster's tail is then driven into the mud and revolved until a hole is scooped out and the victims scraped off the spike and tossed in, whereupon the snoligoster beats them into a batter with its rapidly revolving propeller and inhales them.

Mr. Inman F. Eldredge, of De Funiak Springs, Florida, while hunting for an outlaw negro in the swamps, had a most unusual experience. He caught sight of the negro, dead and impaled upon what at first appeared to be a slender cypress knee, but which presently began to move away. It was then seen to be the spike on a snoligcster's back. Eldredge's first impulse was to shoot the strange beast, but upon second thought he concluded that it was doing a good work and was entitled to live on. The very report of such a creature inhabiting the swamps would deter evil-doers from venturing into these wild places to avoid their pursuers and escape justice.

THE LEPROCAUN

THE LEPROCAUN.
(*Simiidiabolus hibernicus horribilis.*)

During the early days of Upper Canada, before it became the Province of Ontario, there were brought into a logging camp on the Madawaska River several young leprocauns from the north of Ireland. This animal was even then rare and has since become extinct in its native land. It is said that during the last famine hungry Irishmen killed and ate the few remaining specimens of this queer beast.

On its native bogs the leprocaun was a harmless creature, celebrated for its playfulness and laughable antics. It would hop across the bogs, turn somersaults, and leap over hillocks with wondrous agility. A favorite trick was to bore into a pile of drying peat and then, with a sudden spring, send the clods of peat high in the air till the commotion looked like a young cyclone. These antics were all right enough in Ireland, but when the animal was brought to Canada its disposition changed at once. The pets on the Madawaska escaped into nearby tamarack swamps, increasing and spreading until an occasional one was seen on the upper Ottawa and even over in northern Michigan. Sneaking through the tamarack and cedar, or leaping across the muskegs after whatever appealed to it as food, the leprocaun became a creature to be feared and avoided. Teamsters toting supplies across swamp roads have been attacked by the animal, which would bound clear over the load, snapping its teeth at the driver and reaching for him with its villainous claws. Hasty flight to thick timber, leaving the team to its fate, was the only choice of the driver, who thanked his stars that in running through tangled tamarack even the leprocaun is no match for a frightened man.

THE FUNERAL MOUNTAIN TERRASHOT

THE FUNERAL MOUNTAIN TERRASHOT.
(Funericorpus displosissimum.)

This animal explains the origin of the name of the Funeral Range, California. The creature has a casket-like body, six to eight feet long, with a shell running the whole length of its back. Its four legs are long and wobbly, causing the terrashot to sway uncertainly from side to side and forward and back- ward as it travels along.

The strange beast was first reported by some Mormon emigrants, who observed a peculiar procession entering the desert from a certain mountain range, afterward named the Funeral Mountains. They also witnessed the tragic fate of the creatures. One of the Mormons, aroused by his curiosity, made an investigation which resulted in finding out about all that is known of the terrashot. It seems that the animal lives in the little meadows and parks in the higher portions of the range, where it gradually increases in numbers, until by a strange impulse it is seized by a desire to emigrate. They then form long processions and march down into the desert, with the evident intention of crossing to other ranges that can be seen in the distance, but none of them ever gets across. As they encounter the hot sands they rapidly distend with the heat, and one after another they blow up with resounding reports, leaving deep, grave-shaped holes in the sand.

Page Nineteen

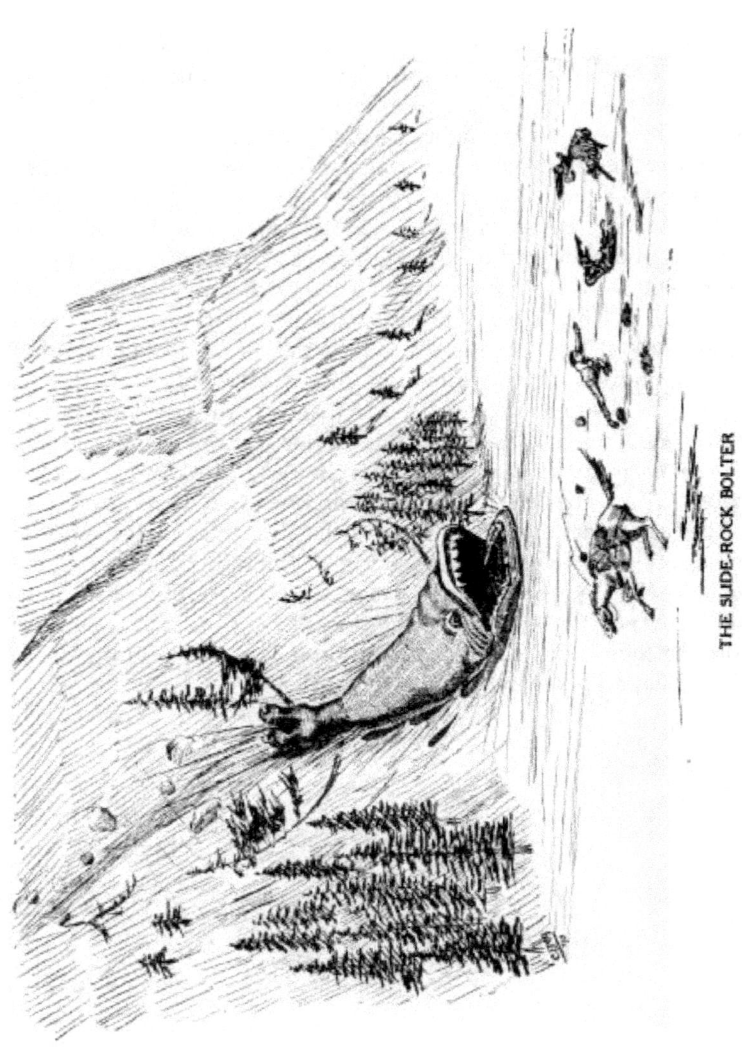

THE SLIDE-ROCK BOLTER

THE SLIDE-ROCK BOLTER.
(Macrostoma saxiperrumptus.)

In the mountains of Colorado, where in summer the woods are becoming infested with tourists, much uneasiness has been caused by the presence of the slide-rock bolter. This frightful animal lives only in the steepest mountain country where the slopes are greater than 45 degrees. It has an immense head, with small eyes, and a mouth somewhat on the order of a sculpin, running back beyond its ears. The tail consists of a divided flipper, with enormous grab-hooks, which it fastens over the crest of the mountain or ridge, often remaining there motionless for days at a time, watching the gulch for tourists or any other hapless creature that may enter it. At the right moment, after sighting a tourist, it will lift its tail, thus loosening its hold on the mountain, and with its small eyes riveted on the poor unfortunate, and drooling thin skid grease from the corners of its mouth, which greatly accelerates its speed, the bolter comes down like a toboggan, scooping in its victim as it goes, its own impetus carrying it up the next slope, where it again slaps its tail over the ridge and waits. Whole parties of tourists are reported to have been gulped at one swoop by the slide-rock bolter, and guides are becoming cautious about taking parties far back into the hills. The animal is a menace not only to tourists but to the woods as well. Many a draw through spruce-covered slopes has been laid low, the trees being knocked out by the roots or mowed off as by a scythe where the bolter has crashed down through from the peaks above.

A forest ranger, whose district includes the rough country between Ophir Peaks and the Lizzard Head, conceived the bold idea of decoying a slide-rock bolter to its own destruction. A dummy tourist was rigged up with plaid Norfolk jacket, knee breeches, and a guide book to Colorado. It was then filled full of giant powder and fulminate caps and posted in a conspicuous place, where, sure enough, the next day it attracted the attention of a bolter which had been hanging for days on the slope of Lizzard Head. The resulting explosion flattened half the buildings in Rico, which were never rebuilt, and the surrounding hills fattened flocks of buzzards the rest of the summer.

Page Twenty-one

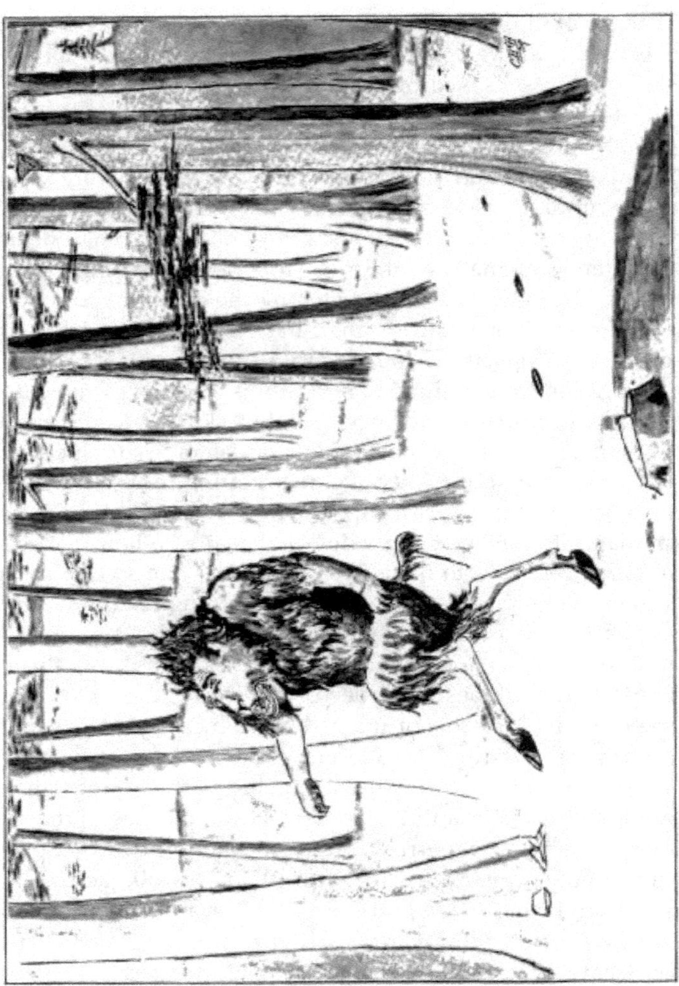

THE TOTE-ROAD SHAGAMAW

THE TOTE-ROAD SHAGAMAW.
(*Bipedester delusissimus.*)

From the Rangeley Lakes to the Allegash and across in New Brunswick loggers tell of an animal which has puzzled many a man, even those who were not strangers in the woods. Frequently the report is circulated that the tracks of a bear have been seen near camp, but a little later this is denied and moose tracks are reported instead. Heated arguments among the men, sometimes resulting in fist lights, are likely to follow. It is rightly considered an insult to a woodsman to accuse him of not being able to distinguish the track of either of these animals. To only a few of the old timber cruisers and rivermen is the explanation of these changing tracks known. Gus Demo, of Oldtown, Maine, who has hunted and trapped and logged in the Maine woods for 40 years, once came upon what he recognized as the tracks of a moose. After following it for about 80 rods it changed abruptly into unmistakable bear tracks; another 80 rods and it changed to moose tracks again. It was soon observed by Mr. Demo that these changes took place precisely every quarter of a mile, and, furthermore, that whatever was making the tracks always followed a tote road or a blazed line through the woods. Coming up within sight of the animal, Gus saw that it had front feet like a bear's and hind feet like those of a moose, and. that it was pacing carefully, taking exactly a yard at a step. Suddenly it stopped, looked all about, and swung as on a pivot, then inverting itself and walking on its front feet only, it resumed its pacing. Mr. Demo was only an instant in recognizing by the witness trees that the place where the animal changed was a section corner. From this fact he reasoned that the shagamaw must have been originally a very imitative animal, which, from watching surveyors, timber cruisers, and trappers patiently following lines through the woods, contracted the habit itself. He figures that the shagamaw can count only as high as 440; therefore it must invert itself every quarter of a mile.

Page Twenty-three

THE WAPALOOSIE

THE WAPALOOSIE.
(Geometrigradus cilioretractus.)

In the damp forests of the Pacific coast and eastward as far as the St. Joe River, in north Idaho, ranges a quaint little beast, known among loggers as the wapaloosie. It is about the size of a sausage dog, but is not even distantly related to the canine family. The wapaloosie, according to lumber jacks, lives upon shelf fungus or conchs exclusively, and he is able to get them with ease, no matter if they are growing on the tip top of a hundred- foot dead tree. It is a pleasure for one of these animals to climb, for he has feet and toes like those of a woodpecker, and he humps himself along like a measuring worm. Even his tail is spiked at the tip and aids him as he mounts the lofty firs in quest of food. One of the most peculiar features of the animal was dis- covered only recently. A lumber jack in one of the camps on the Humptulips River, Washington, shot a wapaloosie, and upon examining its velvety coat decided that it would make an attractive and serviceable pair of mittens, which he proceeded to make. The hide was tanned thoroughly and the mittens made with care, fur side out, and as the lumber jack went to work he exhibited them with pride. Imagine his surprise upon taking hold of an ax to find that the mittens immediately worked their way up and off the handle. It was the same with whatever he took hold of, and, finding that he could not use the mittens, they were left in a skid road, and were last seen working their way over logs and litter across the slashing.

Page Twenty-live

THE CACTUS CAT

THE CACTUS CAT.
(Cactifelinus inebrius.)

How many people have heard of the cactus cat? Thousands of people spend their winters in the great Southwest—the land of desert and mountain, of fruitful valleys, of flat-topped mesas, of Pueblos, Navajos, and Apaches, of sunshine, and the ruins of ancient Cliff-dwellers. It is doubtful, however, if one in a hundred of these people ever heard of a cactus cat, to say nothing of seeing one sporting about among the cholla and palo verde. Only the old-timers know of the beast and its queer habits.

The cactus cat, as its name signifies, lives in the great cactus districts, and is particularly abundant between Prescott and Tucson. It has been reported, also, from the valley of the lower Yaqui, in Old Mexico, and the cholla-covered hills of Yucatan. The cactus cat has thorny hair, the thorns being especially long and rigid on its ears. Its tail is branched, and upon the forearms above its front feet are sharp, knifelike blades of bone. With these blades it slashes the base of giant cactus trees, causing the sap to exude. This is done systematically, many trees being slashed in the course of several nights as the cat makes a big circuit. By the time it is back to the place of beginning the sap of the first cactus has fermented into a kind of mescal, sweet and very intoxicating. This is greedily lapped up by the thirsty beast, which soon becomes fiddling drunk, and goes waltzing off in the moonlight, rasping its bony forearms across each other and screaming with delight.

THE HODAG

THE HODAG.
(Nasobatilus hystrivoratus.)

This animal has been variously described by woodsmen from Wisconsin and Minnesota. Opinions differ greatly as to the appearance of the beast, some claiming it to be covered with horns and spines and having a maniacal disposition. The description which seems most authentic and from which the sketch of the animal has been made is as follows: Size, about that of a rhinoceros and somewhat resembling that animal in general makeup. The creature is slow in motion, deliberate, and, unlike the rhinoceros, very intelligent. Its hairless body is mottled, striped, and checked in a striking manner, suggestive of the origin of the patterns upon Mackinaw clothing, now used in the lumber woods. On the hodag's nose, instead of a horn there is a large spade-shaped bony growth, with peculiar phalanges, extending up in front of the eye, so that he can see only straight up. This probably accounts for the deliberate disposition of the animal, which wanders through the spruce woods looking for suitable food. About the only living creature which the hodag can catch is the porcupine; indeed, it would appear that the porcupine is its natural food. Upon sighting one rolled up in the branches of a spruce the hodag begins to blink his eyes, lick his chops, and spade around the tree, cutting all the roots until the tree begins to totter. He then backs off, and with a rush rams his shovel nose under the roots and over goes the tree, knocking the breath out of the porcupine in its fall. The hodag then straddles the fallen tree, follows it out to the top, where the huge pointed hoofs of its front feet crush the helpless porcupine, and then deliberately swallow-s him head first.

In the autumn the hodag strips the bark off a number of spruce or pine trees and covers himself all over with pitch. He then searches out a patch of hardwood timber where dead leaves lie thick on the ground. Here he rolls about until completely encased in a thick, warm mantle of leaves, in which condition he spends the winter.

THE SQUONK

THE SQUONK.
(Lacrimacorpus dissolvens.)

The range of the squonk is very limited. Few people outside of Pennsylvania have ever heard of the quaint beast, which is said to be fairly common in the hemlock forests of that State. The squonk is of a very retiring disposition, generally traveling about at twilight and dusk. Because of its misfitting skin, which is covered with warts and moles, it is always unhappy; in fact it is said, by people who are best able to judge, to be the most morbid of beasts. Hunters who are good at tracking are able to follow a squonk by its tear-stained trail, for the animal weeps constantly. When cornered and escape seems impossible, or when surprised and frightened, it may even dissolve itself in tears. Squonk hunters are most successful on frosty moonlight nights, when tears are shed slowly and the animal dislikes moving about; it may then be heard weeping under the boughs of dark hemlock trees. Mr. J. P. Wentling, formerly of Pennsylvania, but now at St. Anthony Park, Minnesota, had a disappointing experience with a squonk near Mont Alto. He made a clever capture by mimicking the squonk and inducing it to hop into a sack, in which he was carrying it home, when suddenly the burden lightened and the weeping ceased. Wentling unslung the sack and looked in. There was nothing but tears and bubbles.

Page Thirty-one

THE WHIRLING WHIMPUS

THE WHIRLING WHIMPUS.
(Turbinoccissus nebuloides.)

Occasionally it happens that inexperienced hunters and others wandering in the woods disappear completely. Guides are unable to locate them, and all kinds of theories are offered to explain the disappearances.

From the hardwood forests of the Cumberland Mountains, Tennessee, comes the rumor of an animal called the whirling whimpus, the existence of which may throw some light upon the fate of those who fail to come back to camp. According to woodsmen who have been ^'looking" timber in eastern Tennessee, the whimpus is a blood-thirsty creature of no mean proportions. It has a gorilla-shaped head and body and enormous front feet. Its unique method of obtaining food is to station itself upon a trail, generally at a bend in the trail, where it stands on its diminutive hind legs and whirls. The speed is increased until the animal is invisible, and the motion produces a strange droning sound, seeming to come from the trees overhead. Any creature coming along the trail and not recognizing the sound is almost certain to walk into the danger zone and become instantly deposited in the form of syrup or varnish upon the huge paws of the whimpus.

Page Thirty-three

THE AGROPELTER

THE AGROPELTER.
(*Anthrocephalus craniofractens.*)

Leading a vengeful existence, resenting the intrusion of the logger, the agropelter deals misery to the lumber jack from Maine to Oregon. Ill fares the man who attempts to pass a hollow tree in which one of these creatures has taken up its temporary abode. The unfortunate is usually found smashed or pinned by a dead branch and reported as having been killed by a falling limb. So unerring is the aim of the agropelter that despite diligent search I have been unable to locate more than one man who has been the target for one of their missiles and yet survived to describe the beast. This is Big Ole Kittleson, who, upon a certain occasion, when cruising timber on the upper St. Croix, was knocked down by a partly rotten limb thrown by an agropelter. This limb was so punky that it shattered on Ole's head, and he had time to observe the rascally beast before it bounded from the tree and whisked itself off through the woods.

According to Ole, the animal has a slender, wiry body, the villainous face of an ape, and arms like muscular whiplashes, with which it can snap off dead branches and hurl them through the air like shells from a six-inch gun. It is supposed to feed upon hoot owls and woodpeckers, the scarcity of which will always prevent the agropelter from becoming numerous in any locality.

THE SPLINTER CAT

THE SPLINTER CAT.
(*Felynx arbordiffisus.)*

A widely distributed and frightfully destructive animal is the splinter cat. It is found from the Great Lakes to the Gulf, and eastward to the Atlantic Ocean, but in the Rocky Mountains has been reported from only a few localities. Apparently the splinter cat inhabits that part of the country in which wild bees and raccoons abound. These are its natural food, and the animal puts in every dark and stormy night shattering trees in search of coons or honey. It doesn't use any judgment in selecting coon trees or bee trees, but just smashes one tree after another until a hollow one containing food is found. The method used by this animal in its destructive work is simple but effective. It climbs one tree, and from the uppermost branches bounds down and across toward the tree it wishes to destroy. Striking squarely with its hard face, the splinter cat passes right on, leaving the tree broken and shattered as though struck by lightning or snapped off by the wind. Appalling destruction has been wrought by this animal in the Gulf States, where its work in the shape of a wrecked forest is often ascribed to windstorms.

Page Thirty-Seven

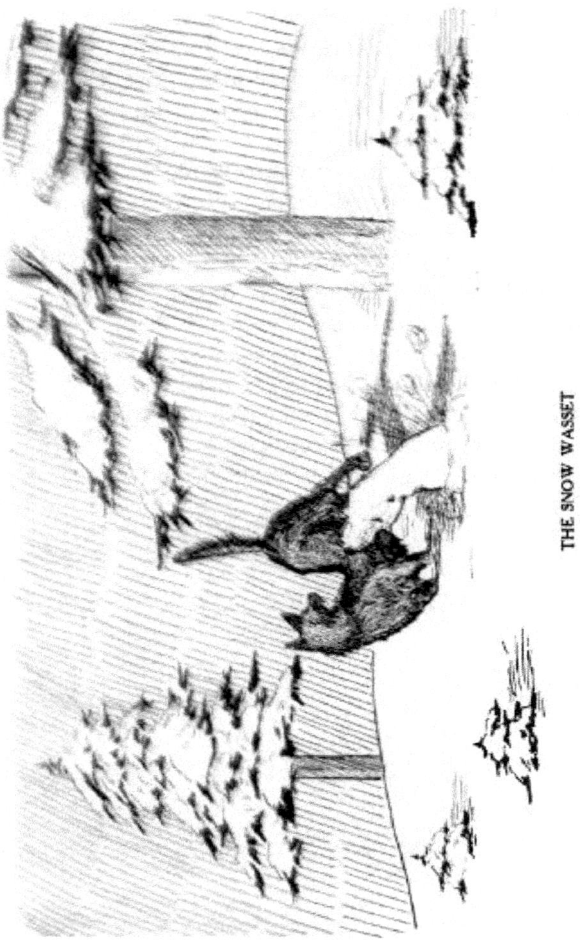

THE SNOW WASSET

THE SNOW WASSET.
(*Mustelinopsis subitivorax.*)

On the most northern logging camps of Canada we hear of the snow wasset. This is surely an animal of the Boreal Zone. It is a migratory animal, wintering in the lumbering region between the Great Lakes and Hudson Bay and spending its summers far north in Labrador and the Barren Grounds. Unlike most wild creatures of the North, the wasset is said to hibernate during only the warmest weather, when its hair turns green and it curls up in a cranberry marsh. During the summer it has rudimentary legs, which enable it to creep slowly around and remain in the shade.

After the first howling snowstorm the wasset sheds its legs and starts south, dipping about in the snow. It soon attains remarkable skill in this method of travel, which enables it to surprise burrowing grouse, crouching rabbits, and skulking varmints of many kinds. Later in the winter, when food becomes scarce and more difficult to obtain, even wolves are seized from below and dragged howling and kicking into the snowdrifts. According to woodsmen, the tragedies of the far North are more numerous beneath the crusted snow than above it. There is no telling how many creatures are pulled down and eaten by the wasset, for this animal has a voracious appetite, comparable only to that of the wolverine, but since it is four times as big and forty times as active as the wolverine it must eat correspondingly more.

The only specimen of this beast ever examined by white men was an imperfect one on James Bay, where a party of surveyors found an Indian in a peculiar canoe, which, upon examination, was shown to be made from one wasset hide greatly stretched. There being no leg holes in the white winter pelt, it is peculiarly adapted to the making of shapely one-man canoes, which are said to be used also as sleds by the Indians. A whole battery of dead-falls are believed to be used in trapping a wasset, since it is impossible to tell in what direction the animal's body may extend. The trigger is set so that a dozen logs fall in from all sides toward the bait, pinning the animal under the snow wherever he may be.

Page Thirty-nine

THE CENTRAL AMERICAN WHINTOSSER

THE CENTRAL AMERICAN WHINTOSSER.
(Cephalovertens semperambulatus.)

In the spring of 1906 there appeared suddenly in the Coast Ranges of California an uncanny animal from the region of the Isthmus. It is not a large beast, but what it lacks m size it makes up in meanness of disposition. None of the lumber jacks who have met a whintosser on trail or tote road care to have the experience repeated. The Central American whintosser is always looking for trouble or making it. In fact the beast seems to be constructed for the purpose of passing through unusual experiences. Its head is fastened to its body by a swivel neck; so is its short, tapering tail; and both can be spun around at the rate of a hundred revolutions a minute. The body is long and triangular, with three complete sets of legs; this is a great convenience in an earthquake country, since the animal is not disturbed by any convulsions of the earth. If the floor suddenly becomes the ceiling it does not matter, for the whintosser is always there with the legs. Its hair is bristly, and all slants forward at a sharp angle. It has been found that a cat's nine lives are as nothing to the one possessed by a whintosser. This animal may be shot, clubbed, or strung on a pike pole without stopping the wriggling, whirling motions or the screams of rage. The only successful way of killing the beast is to poke it into a flume pipe so that all its feet strike the surface, when it immediately starts to walk in three different directions at once and tears itself all apart.

John Gray, of Anadar, Trinity County, California, knows where a pair of whintossers live in some bro ken-up country along Mad River.

Page Forty-one

THE BILLDAD

THE BILLDAD.
(*Saltipiscator falcorostratus.*)

If you have ever paddled around Boundary Pond, in northwest Maine, at night you have probably heard from out the black depths of a cove a spat like a paddle striking the water. It may have been a paddle, but the chances are ten to one that it was a billdad fishing. This animal occurs only on this one pond, in Hurricane Township. It is about the size of a beaver, but has long, kangaroo-like hind legs, short front legs, webbed feet, and a heavy, hawk-like bill. Its mode of fishing is to crouch on a grassy point overlooking the water, and when a trout rises for a bug, to leap with amazing swiftness just past the fish, bringing its heavy, flat tail down with a resounding smack over him. This stuns the fish, which is immediately picked up and eaten by the billdad. It has been reported that sixty yards is an average jump for an adult male.

Up to three years ago the opinion was current among lumber jacks that the billdad was fine eating, but since the beasts are exceedingly shy and hard to catch no one was able to remember having tasted the meat. That fall one was killed on Boundary Pond and brought into the Great Northern Paper Company's camp on Hurricane Lake, where the cook made a most savory slumgullion of it. The first (and only) man to taste it was Bill Murphy, a tote-road swamper from Ambegegis. After the first mouthful his body stiffened, his eyes glazed, and his hands clutched the table edge. With a wild yell he rushed out of the cook-house, down to the lake, and leaped clear out fifty yards, coming down in a sitting posture—exactly like a billdad catching a fish. Of course, he sank like a stone. Since then not a lumber jack in Maine will touch billdad meat, not even with a pike pole.

Page Forty-three

THE TRIPODERO

THE TRIPODERO.
(Collapsofemuris geocatapeltes.)

The chaparral and foothill forests of California contain many queer freaks of one kind and another. One of the strangest and least known is the tripodero, an animal with two contractile or telescopic legs and a tail like a kangaroo's. This peculiarity in structure enables the animal to elevate itself at will, so that it may tower above the chaparral, or, if it chooses, to pull in its legs and present a compact form for crowding through the brush. The tripodero's body is not large but is solidly built, and its head is nearly all snout, the value of which is seen in the method by which food is obtained. As the animal travels through the brush-covered country it elongates its legs from time to time, thus shoving itself up above the brush for purposes of observation. If it sights game within a range of ten rods it takes aim with its snout and tilts itself until the right elevation is obtained, then with astounding force blows a sun-dried quid of clay knocking its victim senseless. (A supply of these quids is always carried in the left jaw.) The tripodero then contracts its legs and bores its way through the brush to its victim, where it stays until the last bone is cracked and eaten.

Page Forty-five

THE HYAMPOM HOG BEAR

Fearsome Creatures of the Lumberwoods

www.ingramcontent.com/pod-product-compliance
Lightning Source LLC
LaVergne TN
LVHW020312110826
845148LV00017BA/2639

* 9 7 8 1 6 6 7 3 0 4 4 1 0 *